THE MUTTSKATEERS

written and illustrated by

Karen Koehler

First Printing

978-1-926898-94-0

Pine Lake Books has allowed this work to remain as the author intended.

The characters in this book are fictionalized accounts of the lives of the author's dogs.

Acknowledgements:

As a youngster I fell in love with the rhythms and rhymes of Theodor Suess Geisel's children's books which were written under the pen name of Dr. Suess. He was my inspiration for the way these stories are written. These stories star our beloved dogs Bundle, Oodle, Much, and Buncho.

Special thanks to my husband who supported me in acquiring and caring for our fur kids, and making sure we can do the activities we love together. Thank you to my family, friends, and the Haliburton Writers club (especially Marie Gage and Brenda Peddigrew). They all encouraged me to write this book and helped with critique. Thanks for my mom for inspiring me to do artwork, and all my English teachers who expressed they enjoyed my writing. Thanks as well to Lynn Simpson who gave me a chance to publish locally and make my dream of publishing books a reality.

Introduction:

Walking our dogs Bundle, Oodle, Much, and Buncho on a lead is not much fun for either us or the dogs, as we just can't go as fast as my dogs want, and our arms get sore because they love to pull. As our property is only a half acre of safe space to play we explore the world attached together, in one way or another, so that I can go as fast as they want, and we can still be together. At my good friends' farms that are far from roads I can let one dog free run while another is attached to me and be quite sure that the free one will stay near me, as we are moving fast enough to be more fun and exciting than the wildlife. The plan is not fool proof, but the more we practice the more confident we get with where each of us is.

While I started to do these activities on my own when I adopted two retired sled dogs that were still very keen to stay active, I began to do races soon after and learned proper techniques and equipment to use. I have now been to five IFSS World Championships, and enjoy teaching people to do these activities with their dogs. GEE and HAW are commands commonly used when working with animals to indicate to them direction. GEE is for right and HAW is for left. I have always used these with my dogs, but in Norway for example they simply use left and right.

The 3 Muttskateers and the 4th

My three mutts with long ears,
they're my Muttskateers,
some I've had for just a few years.

Bundle is six, his colour a mix;
what his tail flicks, it takes time to fix.

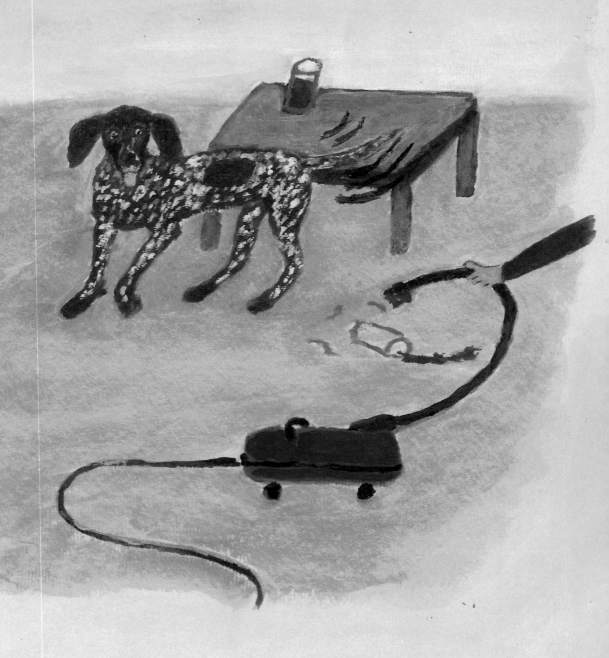

Tell Bundle he's cute, after feeding him fruit.
And now he thinks, "Let's have a hoot."

A full body wag, a big zigzag,
and now he begins the game of tag.

He trundles and stumbles and I end up in tumbles.
In these tumbles, there are mumbles.
They come out in jumbles.

As I lie there like that, flat on my back,
I'm just so glad, I survived that attack.

Bundle likes to whine and pine,
especially when it is time to dine,

but most of all before run time.

10

With bundles of energy he will spin to and fro,
and all I can say is:
"NO, please WHOA!"

I hook him up, I get behind,
now it's time for him to unwind!

He can't wait to RUN, to run for fun,
under the sun, as we become one.

Oodle is four, he bounds at the door.
He loves to chase bugs,

...and loves to get hugs!

He's not that big, and likes to dig.

At night he likes to huddle and cuddle.

When he crushes my toes, I plan my rebuttal.

For just one moment he's lazy as a daisy,
but that moment gone, the next one he's crazy!

Did I say ...

CRAZY!

Oodle will notice as I grab my skis.
But will it be possible to even wear these.

With oodles of energy he bounds to and fro.
And all I can say is:
"NO, please WHOA!"

I can't hook him up, I can't get behind.

Then finally the point, he gets to unwind.

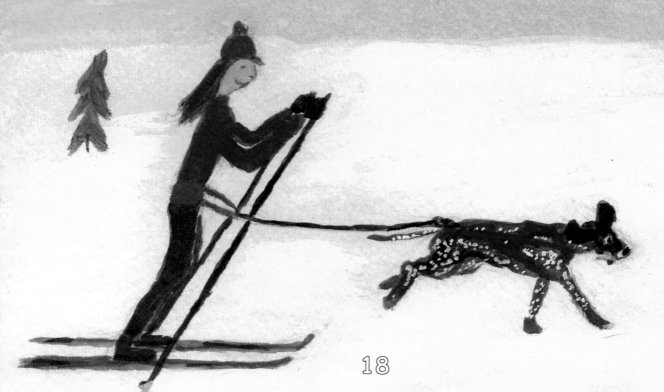

18

He can't wait to run, to run for fun,
under the sun, as we become one.

Much is BIG and he is two,
and really he is quite very new;

He has a white blaze
and a steady strong gaze,
polka spot speckles,
and black and white freckles!

And even though Much has a very soft touch,
he really can be, much too much.

As I lie deep in sleep,
he will make a peep.

And so I say,
before I hit the hay,
to Much on the couch,
in his comfortable slouch,

"It's time to pee."
But Much rolls over and pictures a tree.
He goes on his back, and is filled with glee,
as I sit beside him on my knee.

After some cuddles a push and shove,
his paws touch the ground light as a dove.

He does a big stretch, I open the latch,
now ready to fetch, he goes out to catch!

He waters the tree, with lots of pee!
Now sure to be, some sleep for me!

Sweet dreams of weather,
hope for the better,
maybe dryer, maybe wetter.

24

A run in the sun, a run after dark,
no matter which one, there's sure to be bark, barK,
BARK.

I hook him up, and get behind.

Now he too, gets to unwind.

Now fun in the dark,
in the dark, darK, DARK,
and luckily no more
bark, barK, BARK!

Now fun in the sun!
He can't wait to RUN, to run for fun,
under the sun, as we become one.

The three mutts with long ears,
my three Muttskateers,
some I've had for just a few years.

Oh my goodness there's more.

It's Buncho, the fourth,
he's also with me, up here in the north.

Buncho is one and full of fun.

He's all brown, can be a clown,
he even loves to chew on down.

He likes to bounce high, he likes to bounce low, he's even been known to pounce on a toe!

This bouncing and pouncing is very real,
next he'll be needing another meal!

One dish, two fish, more food,
SPLISH;
fish in a dish to bounce like this.

We will let that food settle
and run for a medal!

Medals are fun, when they can be won!

But best is to RUN, to run for fun,
under the sun, as we become one.

33

The three Muttskateers and the fourth!
Fun in the sun even up north!

In this moment and that moment,
I love every moment
with my mutts with long ears,
my Muttskateers.

The Muttskateers and the Golden Nugget

One Saturday, the three Muttskateers and the fourth
meet a dog in a town just up north.

They sniff a hello with a nod from mums.
They even sniff their tailed bums.

A golden nugget hangs from its collar,
it seems to make that dog stand taller.

The nugget sparkles golden, golden in the sun.
How much fun, to wear a nugget,
a golden nugget in the sun.

And at that moment they part ways.
That just so happens on some of those days.

At home its owner sits in a chair.
She just doesn't really seem to care.

She does her hair, and eats a pear.
She doesn't even think to share.

She puts down her comb and gets out her phone.
Now things are quite, seriously, monotone.

And now that dog will slouch on the couch,
and lay that way for most of the day.

The dog's nose upon that nugget,
with her paw she will tug it,
but no longer golden will be the nugget.

Her eyes will close and she will doze,
lying sadly on a pile of clothes.

The three Muttskateers and the 4th,
go to a training spot just up north.

A safe spot far from cars and from roads,
but they are quite sure they will see some toads.

They like to be at that spot a lot.

Two mutts with long ears
get their turn to sing cheers.
They bark their cheers, with bouncing ears.

The sight of the bike is something they like.

Bundle will trundle with not a stumble.

And at the end he will have a fun tumble!

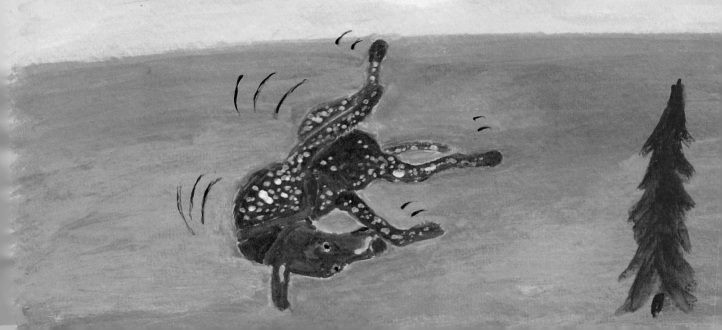

As Bundle trundles,
Buncho will bounce, bounce, BOUNCE.

He will bounce and bounce and then he'll POUNCE.

43

Fun in the sun; as they run as one.
Those dogs in the sun, in the sun with their mum!

And Buncho looks for a nugget,
because that nugget looked fun.
He too wants a golden nugget to wear in the sun.

It must bring compassion, as well as fun fashion!

It must bring peace,
as good as the silence after chasing the geese.

Buncho looks high and he looks low.

But no nugget is to be found,
by the brown Buncho.

Now two more mutts get a turn to explore,
this is definitely something that they will adore.

Oodle looks lazy,
but just wait he's crazy.

He'll pull that scooter under the sun,
if he will be patient and wait for mum.
Much is all ready to have some fun.

This could be bad. Mom might be mad,
if she survives this lesson she will be glad!

Never trust that Much, mutt like that,
for he may mislead Oodle after that cat.

Mom brushes off,
after the sit on her toff.

She knows her mistake, time for retake!
This time she's ready to avoid the lake!

PHEW!

Fun in the sun, as they run as one!
Those dogs in the sun, in the sun with their mum!

Much also looks for a nugget,
because that nugget looked fun.
He too wants a golden nugget to wear in the sun.

It must bring joy, like a favourite play toy!
It must be magic, not found will be tragic.

The dogs get to run. They get to help mum.
They get to be free and listen for GEE!
And sometimes HAW,

... then it's time, to shake a paw.

But still no nugget to show to ma.

Now it's Canicross for Much on the moss.
How much field will they cross?
And who will, really, be the boss?

And it's Bundle's turn now, for him to run free.
He is sure to listen for mum to say "GEE!"

Fun in the sun;
as they run as one!
Those dogs in the sun,
in the sun with their mum!

Bundle looks for a nugget,
because that nugget looked fun.
He too wants a golden nugget to wear in the sun.

It must grant wishes as good as full dishes.

It must make dreams come true,
sure as the feeling of I love woooo!

Bundle looks far and wide, he even looks side to side.
But he cannot find where such a nugget might hide.

"Now what to do? Buncho you must pull too!
Here is a cart just perfect for you."

Buncho pulls now with a bounce, bounce, bounce,
and kindly he does not even pounce!

Oodle runs free! He is filled
with glee!
He may possibly listen, if
mum says, "Gee!"

Fun in the sun; as they run as one!
Those dogs in the sun, in the sun with their mum!

Oodle looks for a nugget,
because that nugget looked fun.
He too wants a golden nugget to wear in the sun.

Such a special thing, what qualities it must bring;
happiness and laughter, and all that sort of thing.

Oodle looks all through the marsh, but the facts are harsh.
Such nuggets cannot be found in that sort of marsh.

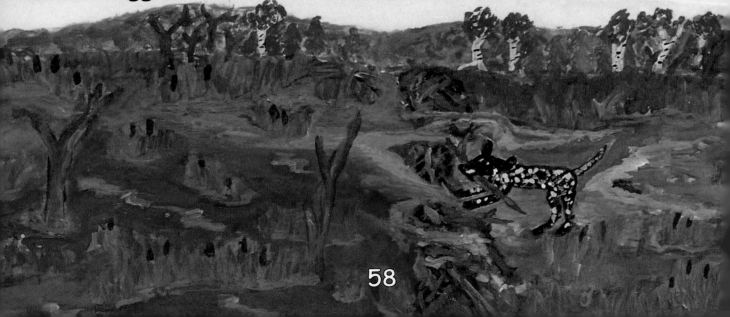

And when day is done and they sit in the sun,
no nugget to find, perhaps it was won;
the last golden rays break through the haze,
and cast upon them a very warm glaze.

A day full of adventure, friendship, and play,
together in the sun, they sit that way.

No need for a nugget, it's really no fun.
For the *real* golden nugget is fun in the sun.

Karen Koehler fell in love with skijoring when she and her husband adopted a retired sled dog that still loved to pull. Now she is an advocate for getting individuals and families outdoors and active with their dogs in harness. Done with proper knowledge and care, harness dog activities can be fun for all involved. With 14 years in the sport of competitive skijoring, outdoor adventure activity leadership since 1997, and 12 years of elementary school teaching, Karen now teaches harness dog activities through Yours Outdoors in the Haliburton Highlands area of Ontario, where she lives with her husband and 4 beloved dogs. She has also had a long time passion for creative writing and art.

Bikejor with Oodle (above)
courtesy of Echo Image Photography

Scootering with Bundle (below)
courtesy of Laurel Turansky

Canicross with Bundle (below)
courtesy of Robert Sargent

Karen enjoys outdoor activities with her four muttskateers

Kicksledding with Buncho and Oodle (side)
courtesy of Joey Ouellette

Skijoring with Much and Oodle (above)
courtesy of Marie Parent

Skijoring with Much
courtesy of Daniel Knight Photography

Skijoring with Bundle and Buncho, courtesy of Kaitlynn Paquette (above left)
ikejoring with Oodle, courtesy of Born 2 Run Photography (above right)

Bikejoring with Much

courtesy of Sophie Desbiens Photography and Design

Rob [my super amazing supporter in all things] and Oodle in Germany, courtesy of Frank Eckermann

Karen and all her Dogs

courtesy of Robert Sargeant

Made in the USA
Middletown, DE
22 September 2019